Best Friends

Learning Simple Shapes

by Lynn Maslen Kertell
pictures by Sue Hendra and John R. Maslen

Scholastic Inc.
New York • Toronto • London • Auckland • Sydney • Mexico City • New Delhi • Hong Kong • Buenos Aires

Sally, a circle, was best friends
with a square named Seth.

Wherever Sally went, Seth went too.
Whatever Sally liked, Seth liked too.

One day, a triangle named Tanner
moved in next door. Soon Sally, Seth,
and Tanner were three good friends.

Until morning, Sally liked
one thing, but Seth and Tanner
liked something different.

Sally felt sad. She gave
herself a sorry hug.

Seth and Tanner searched for Sally, but she was no longer a circle. Her friends didn't recognize her.

Seth and Tanner missed Sally. Seth slumped down. Tanner was upset.

All three started to cry, and
out came tears shaped like
squares, triangles, and circles.

When Sally saw the shapes of the tears, she laughed until she felt she would burst. And look! She was a circle again.

When Seth and Tanner saw her,
they perked up and giggled too.

Sally, Seth, and Tanner
were themselves again—
three good friends.